Trucks

Jill McDougall

Contents

What Trucks Do

Trucks are vehicles.
They can be small, big or very big!

People can do lots of jobs with trucks.

Small trucks can move things
like boxes and tables.

Some trucks can tow away cars
that have broken down.

Big trucks can move lots of cars all at once.

Firefighters need big trucks to help put out fires.

Sometimes, very big trucks can move houses!

Small Trucks

Lots of jobs can be done
with small trucks.

At the **airport**, small trucks
move the planes from place to place.

Sometimes, the trucks push the planes, so they are near to the **runway**. Then, the plane can take off.

Some trucks are **rubbish** trucks.

These trucks are not very big,
but sometimes they need to move big loads.
They can pick up rubbish outside shops,
houses and schools.

The arm on a rubbish truck
can lift up a rubbish bin.
The rubbish falls into the back of the truck.

A rubbish truck is always needed
to lift big, heavy bins.

Big Trucks

Some trucks are very big.

Tip trucks are big trucks
that can move loads of sand and rock.

The back of a tip truck can lift up,
so the load will slide onto the ground.

Tip trucks have big engines
because they have big loads to move.

The back lifts up.

The load slides out.

Some trucks are very long.
They are called road trains.

Road trains can take heavy loads
a long way.

A road train has a lot of trailers.

Some road trains can have 100 wheels, or more!

Rescue Trucks

Some trucks are rescue trucks.
These trucks can be big or small.

Fire trucks are rescue trucks.
They have water inside them.
Firefighters need the water
to help put out the fires.

Fire trucks can be called fire engines, too.

When a car has broken down on the road,
a tow truck can take it away.

The truck tows the car
to a place where it can be fixed.

If a car or truck gets stuck in mud or snow,
a tow truck must pull it out.

Trucks can be small or big.
People need trucks every day
to move things from place to place.

Glossary

airport a place people go to catch a plane

rubbish things that are not wanted anymore

runway a long strip of ground at an airport where planes take off and land

Trucks

Text: Jill McDougall
Publisher: Eliza Webb
Editor: Annabel Smith
Project editor: Jarrah Moore
Project designer: James Steer
Designer: MAPG
Permissions researcher: Liz McShane
Production controller: Alice Kane
Reprint: Siew Han Ong

Acknowledgements
We would like to thank the following for permission to reproduce copyright material:

Front cover, p. 9: iStock.com/Pro-syanov; p. 2, back cover: iStock.com/XiXinXing; p. 3: Alamy Stock Photo/Justin Kase z12z; pp. 4–5: Dreamstime.com/Dmitri Maruta; p. 6: Alamy Stock Photo/Carmen K. Sisson/Cloudybright; p. 7: Alamy Stock Photo/Tony Miller; pp. 10–11: Dreamstime.com/Andreas Demel; pp. 12–13: Alamy Stock Photo /Ashley Cooper; p. 14: Shutterstock.com/Maryia_K; p. 15: Shutterstock.com/M2020; p. 16 (top): Getty Images/Crocodile Images, (middle): Shutterstock.com/muratart, (bottom): iStock.com/choice76; back cover (background pattern): Shutterstock.com/sahua d.

Every effort has been made to trace and acknowledge copyright. However, if any infringement has occurred, the publishers tender their apologies and invite the copyright holders to contact them.

PM Guided Reading
Orange Level 15

The Dinosaur Chase
A Present for Bella
That Goat Must Go!
Toby and BJ
Toby and the Big Tree
Cassie's Crutches
Gia's New School
Pterosaur's Long Flight
Tiger Cat and Tabby Cat
Guinea Pigs
Cats
Dogs
Making a Shadow Puppet
The Fun House
Trucks

ISBN 978 0 17 032821 0

Cengage Learning Australia
Level 5 , 80 Dorcas Street
Southbank VIC 3006
Phone: 1300 790 853
Email: aust.nelsonprimary@cengage.com

For learning solutions, visit cengage.com.au

Printed in China by 1010 Printing International Ltd
3 4 5 6 7 24 23

1
2
3
4
5
6
7
8
9
10
11
12
13
14
15
16
17
18
19
20
21
22
23
24
25
26
27
28
29
30

Trucks are vehicles. There are small trucks and big trucks. People can do lots of jobs with trucks.

Information Report

Level 15